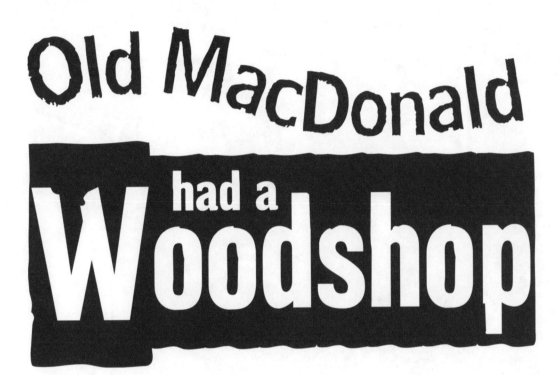

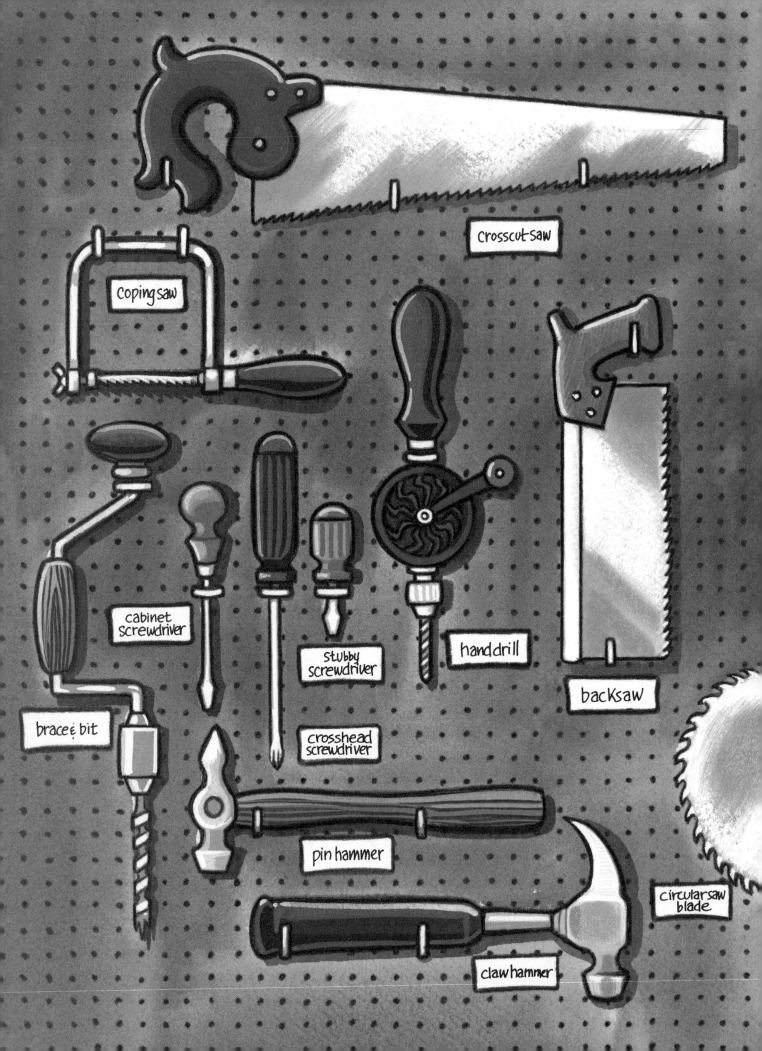

To Paul, Evvy, Mariah, and my mother, Marilyn Shulman.
With love here, and love there, E-I-E-I-O! —L. S.

For Prindle Wissler, who helped me learn to see. —A. W.

ISBN 0-439-73567-X

Text copyright © 2002 by Lisa Shulman. Illustrations copyright © 2002 by Ashley Wolff.
All rights reserved. Published by Scholastic Inc., 557 Broadway, New York, NY 10012, by arrangement with G.P. Putnam's Sons, an imprint of Penguin Putnam Books for Young Readers, a division of Penguin Group (USA) Inc. SCHOLASTIC and associated logos are trademarks and/or registered trademarks of Scholastic Inc.

12 11 10 9 8 7 6 5 4 3 2 1   5 6 7 8 9/0

Printed in the U.S.A.   40

First Scholastic printing, January 2005

Designed by Marikka Tamura. Text set in ITC Cushing.

The art was done on Arches Cover in gouache and pastel with brown-colored pencil line.

Old MacDonald had a Woodshop

LISA SHULMAN

Illustrated by

ASHLEY WOLFF

SCHOLASTIC INC.
New York Toronto London Auckland Sydney
Mexico City New Delhi Hong Kong Buenos Aires

Old MacDonald had a
SHOP,
E-I-E-I-O!

And in her shop she had a

SAW,

E-I-E-I-O!

With a *zztt zztt* here
and a *zztt zztt* there,

here a *zztt,*
there a *zztt,*
everywhere a *zztt zztt.*

Old MacDonald had a shop, E - I - E - I - O.

And in her shop she had a

DRILL,

E-I-E-I-O!

With a *rurr rurr* here
and a *rurr rurr* there,

a *zztt zztt* here
and a *zztt zztt* there,

here a *zztt,* there a *zztt,* everywhere a *zztt zztt.*

Old MacDonald had a shop, E - I - E - I - O .

And in her shop she had a
HAMMER,
E-I-E-I-O!

With a *tap tap* here
and a *tap tap* there,

a *rurr rurr* here
and a *rurr rurr* there,

a *zztt zztt* here
and a *zztt zztt* there,

here a *zztt*, there a *zztt*, everywhere a *zztt zztt*.

Old MacDonald had a shop, E - I - E - I - O.

And in her shop she had a

CHISEL,

E-I-E-I-O!

With a *chip chip* here
and a *chip chip* there,

a *tap tap* here
and a *tap tap* there,

a *rurr rurr* here
and a *rurr rurr* there,

a *zztt zztt* here
and a *zztt zztt* there,

here a *zztt,* there a *zztt,* everywhere a *zztt zztt.*

Old MacDonald had a shop, E - I - E - I - O.

And in her shop she had a
FILE,
E-I-E-I-O!

With a *scritch scratch* here
and a *scritch scratch* there,

a *chip chip* here
and a *chip chip* there,

a *tap tap* here
and a *tap* OUCH! there,

a *rurr rurr* here
and a *rurr rurr* there,

a *zztt zztt* here
and a *zztt zztt* there,

here a *zztt*,
there a *zztt*,
everywhere a *zztt zztt*.

Old MacDonald had a shop, E-I-E-I-O.

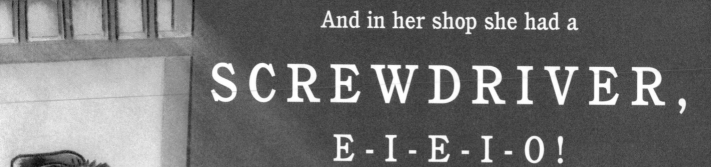

And in her shop she had a

SCREWDRIVER,

E-I-E-I-O!

With a *squeak squeak* here
and a *squeak squeak* there,

a *scritch scratch* here
and a *scritch scratch* there,

a *chip chip* here
and a *chip chip* there,

a *tap tap* here
and a *tap tap* there,

a *rurr rurr* here
and a *rurr rurr* there,

a *zztt zztt* here
and a *zztt zztt* there,

here a *zztt*, there a *zztt*, everywhere a *zztt zztt*.

Old MacDonald had a shop, E - I - E - I - O.

And in her shop she had a

PAINTBRUSH,
E-I-E-I-O!

With a *swish swash* here
and a *swish swash* there,

a *squeak squeak* here
and a *squeak squeak* there,

a *scritch scratch* here
and a *scritch scratch* there,

a *chip chip* here
and a *chip chip* there,

a *tap tap* here
and a *tap tap* there,

a *rurr rurr* here
and a *rurr rurr* there,

a *zztt zztt* here
and a *zztt zztt* there,

here a *zztt*, there a *zztt*, everywhere a *zztt zztt*.

Old MacDonald had a
SHOP,
E-I-E-I-O!

And in her shop she had a . . .

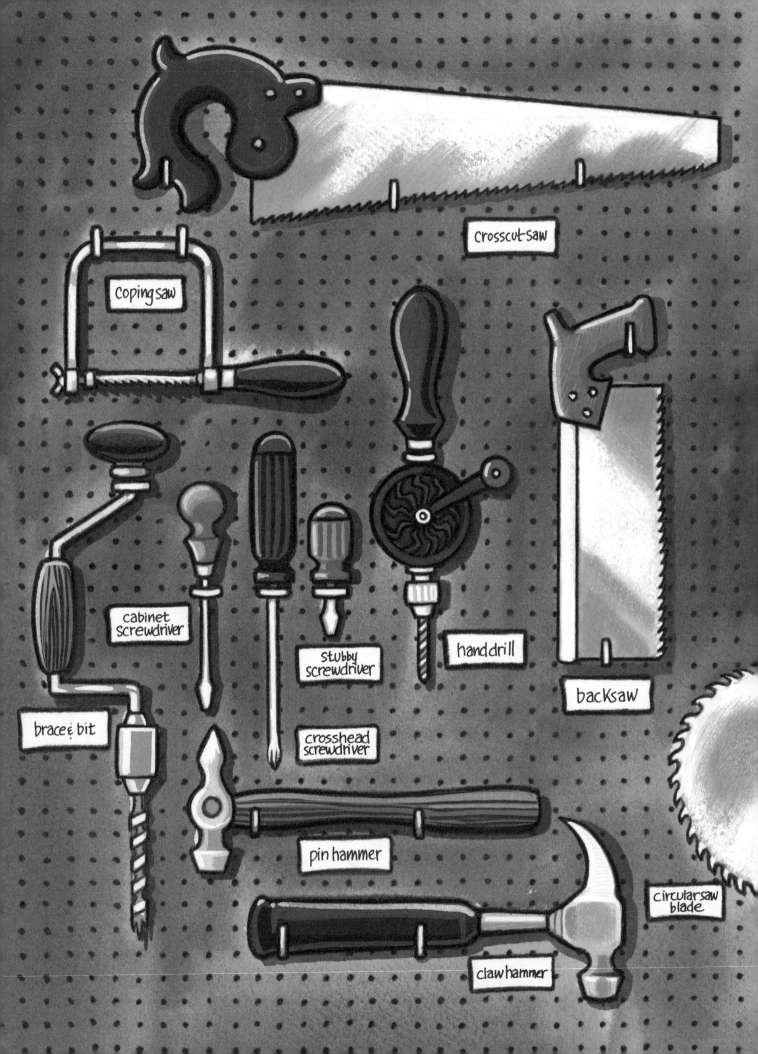

crosscut saw

coping saw

cabinet screwdriver

stubby screwdriver

hand drill

backsaw

brace & bit

crosshead screwdriver

pin hammer

circular saw blade

claw hammer

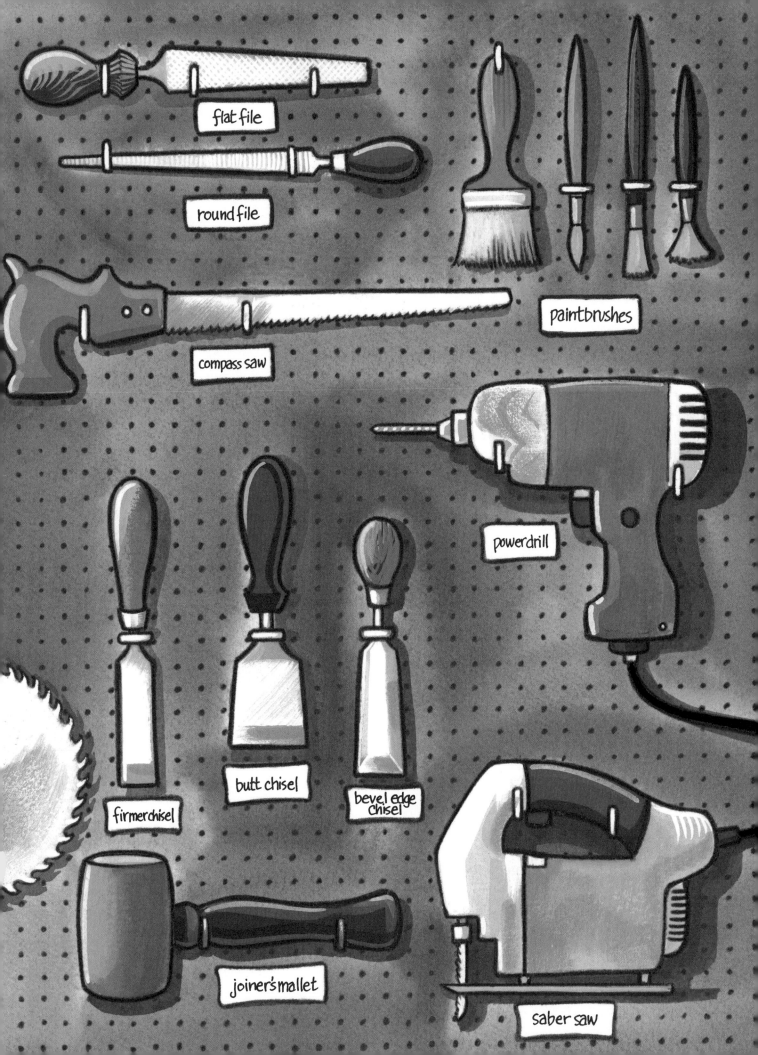

flat file

round file

compass saw

paintbrushes

powerdrill

firmer chisel

butt chisel

bevel edge chisel

joiner's mallet

saber saw